Library of Congress Cataloging-in-Publication Data:
Ross, Katharine, 1950– . Sweetie and Petie / by Katharine Ross ; Illustrated by Lisa McCue. p. cm.—(A Just right book) SUMMARY: A girl skunk preoccupied with her doll and a boy skunk who loves to play pirates find that when they get together they share more interests than they thought. ISBN: 0-394-89864-8 (trade); 0-394-99864-2 (lib. bdg.) [1. Skunks—Fiction. 2. Sex role—Fiction. 3. Play—Fiction.] I. McCue, Lisa, ill. II. Title. III. Series: Just right book (New York, N.Y.) PZ7.R719693Sw 1988 [E]—dc19 87-35434

Manufactured in the United States of America 1 2 3 4 5 6 7 8 9 0

JUST RIGHT BOOKS is a trademark of Random House, Inc.

A Just Right Book

SWEETIE AND PETIE

By Katharine Ross
Illustrated by Lisa McCue

Random House 🏠 New York

Once upon a time, on a little desert island, there was a little skunk named Sweetie. She lived with her father and mother in a hut made of palm fronds.

Sweetie liked to make sand cakes
and then watch the waves lap in and
melt them into sandy goop.

She liked to strum her ukulele and sing songs that she had made up about mermaids and princesses and even pirates.

But best of all, she liked to play with Leilani. Leilani was a very special doll that her father had made for her out of a hollowed-out coconut shell and dried husks. Sweetie liked to comb her hair and dress her and burp her when she got cranky. Leilani wasn't a very pretty doll, but when Sweetie held Leilani in her arms, Sweetie felt very soft and warm inside.

Down the beach from Sweetie, there lived another little skunk, whose name was Petie. Petie liked to shinny up palm trees.

He liked to slide down the waterfall
and tumble—*ker-plosh!*—into the
purple lagoon.

But best of all, he liked to play pirates. His very best toy was a sword his mother had made for him out of an old oar. It wasn't a very sharp sword, but when he held it in his hand, Petie felt very brave.

Sweetie's father and mother were forever trying to get her to go play with Petie. Just as Petie's father and mother were forever trying to get him to go play with Sweetie. But neither was about to have anything to do with the other.

"He's a *boy*," said Sweetie.

"She's a *girl*," said Petie.

One day, Sweetie was bored with making the same old sand cakes. So she took Leilani for a walk down the beach.

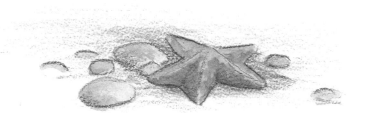

She saw Petie digging in the sand. He didn't look so bad to her.

"Want to see my doll?" she asked. "Her name is Leilani."

Now, it so happened that Petie was just about to start a rousing game of pirates.

"Want to see my ship?" he asked.

"Oh, boy!" said Sweetie, climbing aboard. "This is just like the ship in my song! I'll play the pirate princess and you can be my prisoner."

"Can Leilani play?" asked Petie.

"She would love to," said Sweetie. "She even has a pirate outfit."

Sweetie showed Petie how to dress Leilani and how to comb her hair and how to burp her if she got cranky.

Petie showed Sweetie how to cast off and how to swab a deck and how to walk the plank.

And that was how Sweetie and Petie finally got together. And they have remained friends to this very day.